Inside the Whale

Inside the Whale

A NOVEL IN VERSE

Joseph G. Peterson

Drawings by
MICHAEL BREHM

WICKER PARK PRESS

Inside the Whale
Published by
Wicker Park Press Ltd
P.O. BOX 5318
River Forest, Illinois 60305-5918
WWW.WICKERPARKPRESS-31BOOKS.COM
© 2012 Joseph G. Peterson

ISBN-10: 1-936-67901-9
ISBN-13: 978-1-936679-01-0

LIBRARY OF CONGRESS CONTROL NUMBER: 2011921654

PUBLISHER: Eric Lincoln Miller
EDITOR: Tracy Schoenle
COVER PAINTING: Jon Langford
COVER DESIGN: Michael Brehm
BOOK DESIGN & DRAWINGS: Michael Brehm

Characters in this book are a work of fiction and come from the imagination of
the author. Any similarities to any persons living are dead is a coincidence.

Printed and bound in the United States of America

♾ The paper used in this publication meets the minimum
requirements of the American National Standard for information
Sciences—Permanence of Paper for Printed Library Materials.

for those with whom I have sailed

in shambling family unit

through these years . . .

(peace & love)

PART I

~~~

he was jim
an irishman a rogue
        first generation american
        though once or twice he faked it with a brogue

catholic
second of five children
        rebel child he twice nearly died
        once in a fire of his own making:

at twelve he fell asleep drunk on beer in bed
        when the cigarette he had been smoking (lucky strike)
        lit the pillow near his head

he awoke in a blaze of fire
　　doesn't know what happened next
　　but was told by his older brother, chris,

who saved him from the crisis
　　that he was pinned beneath his bike
gasping for breath and the fire was all about him

　　chris found him there dying
wrapped him in wet towels and pulled him from the fire

　　a scar on his chest
　　　　in the shape of a turtle remains
　　　　and a story in the fashion of a poem
that he published
to some small acclaim a decade later:

i see the turtle in its shell
making its long way 'cross the sand
it leaves its leather egg case behind
and follows the moonlit band to the sea
preyed on by gulls, crows, foxes
it doesn't live by very good chances
i watch it make its turtle walk
it pauses at a hole
should it walk around
but no it tumbles down
helpless
pulled by gravity
it lays on its back
its legs flailing

i too have a turtle
imprinted to my chest
a tattoo of my failing
i earned it in a burning
(i was only twelve at the time)
i'm preyed upon by things:
bad dreams, a penchant for lying, mendacity,
i walk a turtle waddle live
beneath a shell
pass a bottle around
like a turtle i'll come tumbling down

another time jim nearly died while drunk on gin
          doing seventy down the highway

he was twenty-three a poet after the fashion
          of his hero, dylan thomas,
                    a girl, anne, was in the car with jim

          he liked to drink and cuss

          but what's more he liked an audience
                    preferably one he could fuck
                    anne was all he needed

he was telling anne how
he was going to be a great poet one day
when he smashed into the rear of a slow-moving truck

anne died of internal injuries
but jim survived
it was luck that saved him
he even wrote a poem of it:

like a moth
i have fluttered near the white light
   felt its terrible allure
   the terrible allure of letting go
   the terrible allure
   of being done with it
   the terrible allure
   of saying farewell to all that

farewell to clocks and men and things
to those who tell us
what to be
farewell to the need
of being
something
someone

farewell
to being

a voice like a gong sounded
   told me no
   i wasn't done yet
   was still wanted
   for what, though, i wasn't told

and that has ever since been the rub

jim never knew why or for what
he was picked to survive and not anne

    why he was sent back down
    but anne was taken

    he only knew that he was told to do
    but to do what was the question

    he wished ever after

that voice that sounded like a gong
had given him a mission to help him along

perhaps his mission was to give up drink
so he tried a.a. told his tale of woe

vowed abstinence
wrote a series of poems
was dry six months
but still he couldn't let go the bottle
drinking was a struggle with the devil
that's the gist of what jim wrote—when he was writing—
     blind pie-eyed drunk he wrote it
     he wrote it sober
     jim preferred blank verse to rhyming
     he wrote it all down unrehearsed
     then declaimed it drunk
     sometimes it was a thing of beauty
     sometimes it stunk:

if it were me and anyone else
 i would win
 i'm for a fight
  i'll tell you that
 i'm determined
   i've licked more than i know
    it's proven
 but the bottle's a devil by god
  and we're locked in a hold
  he's got me in a clinch
  i've got him half nelson
 it's a fair fight so far
   but it won't remain so long
    as i'm fighting the devil
    and he won't let go his hold.

sometimes in imaginary bouts
jim won sometimes the devil

in the end, though,
jim wished more than anything
the devil would just end this thing and beat him

there was also the problem of anne
who was she anyway
jim didn't know
someone he met at the bar
a potential one night stand
she had lovely hands told him he was romantic
what's more she loved the concept: a poet

flaxen haired is how he described her
in a poem that snowy night
he produced it from a vacuum   *ex-nihilo*
quoted it to her drunk:

you are flaxen haired and the night is long
soldiers plunder their dead

they lie in their fields
             pockets turned out

their eyes stopper the gas
             that builds—builds—inside of them

             why did they leave home
so young for the trenches

why did they leave home so young
             when the flaxen haired girl told them: no,

don't go, my hair is flaxen
the night is long, stay home

she loved the poem
fell for it
>it was a neat trick
>jim with eyes turned back
>summoning the muse

he seemed to pull poems from the ether
like a ferret pulling a rabbit from a hole
didn't know where they came from either

who wrote it, she asked him
have a beer, he said
tell me is it wilfred owen
or siegfried sassoon
or earlier than that
tell me please
is it walt whitman in his civil war phase

have a beer, he said, sit down i'll tell you more
>she was easy to impress
>he was all for impressing
he quoted another direct from memory
but not before having a drink:

i see them all
i see them standing about
as if they were awaiting
the last judgment
so amusing is one that he stands out
cracking jokes
he points his crooked finger at me
the crowd turns and looks
be stained, he says accusingly,
be stained by what you have done
but what have i done? i asked
and while they stood judging me i pleaded:
i have done nothing
and that's when he with the finger said:
exactly and let that be your sentence

it's wonderful, she said
placing her hand on his leg
who is it
is it john donne
or blake

gaze into the tunnels of my eyes and be lost
in a windblown world of breaking hopes
and a shipwrecked country
of green-blue dreams. . . .

nor does jim remember how
anne ended up in his car that night
doesn't know why she was there with him

she was a grad student in literature soon to be a teacher
she wasn't even a drinker
never touched a drop
but a friend had taken her to the bar
    urged her to loosen up
    that's when she saw jim
jim saw her
and something happened

    he offered her a beer
    she resisted
    still he persisted

her friend nudged her
said: loosen up, have some fun

would it surprise you flaxen anne if i said
you sing to me a siren call
i hear you singing like the muse
today we're starting out but
who knows where this will take us
will it take us across the decades
or will it merely take us across town
to a motel perhaps or perhaps to another bar

the shadow that falls between us
the shadow of indifference
i feel it parting
it's rending
it's rending fast

by night's end he could barely stand
she was drunk too

but still
she helped him to his car
                are you ok to drive, she asked
i'm fine
it's not far
just across town
what's more i'm an expert at driving drunk
she got in beside him
watched the snow falling down
                it's snowing, she said
                the streetlights blinked in the snowfall
he likened their reflection in the snow
to halos

it seemed an innocent image that gave her confidence
breath steamed out of them
           where are we going? she asked
              my friend is waiting for me at the bar
don't worry
a little drive
it won't be far

are you ok to drive

        shall i quote you another poem
          about drink and inspiration
          the one is a snake
          the other a lizard
he attempted to summon another poem but was silent
and drove off into the blizzard

the dark country road
the dark winding road
                    wound out of town through the dark mazy
woods
deer poked around in the shoulder of the winding road
the woods were a maze of tree branches cloaked in snow
wiper blade scraped
    defroster broke
    windshield fogged
    at one point
    doing twenty
    at another
    doing seventy
    impossible to keep
    a steady speed
    snow falling
    dropping in clumps
    from branches
    the branches falling
beneath the clumps
    into the soft fallen snow
    falling in the dark woods

the long country road
winds solitary through the maze and thicket
he reaches for a lighter
misses
touches her thigh
she yields a brief sigh

                                    followed by a compressed scream
he doesn't know

                                    whether to veer left or right
of the yellow warning light

                                    goes straight instead
                                    plows into a plow
now she's dead

the last she was touched
alive

                        was by jim

anne burroughs: 1953–1975

~~~

jim listened to the ambulance siren
      nodded off while it bumped through town
      slept a while
and while he slept
had a vision

he walked in yellow wellington boots
                  hand in hand with anne
                  through a field of white flowers
                  orioles in the bowers
in the distance was the sea
(he'd never seen the sea before
but in his vision sees
the endless stretch of saltwater sea dazzling
in the sunlight)

it was there in the field
in sight of the sea
hand in hand with anne
          he felt it
it was the closest
he'd ever come, so far,
(vision or no) to bliss

anne stepped round him, naked, paused
gave him a kiss, found his shaft, smiled
hey, she said, let's not forget this!
          they commenced fornicating
out in the green grass
               the endless stretch of saltwater sea
                    dazzling in the sunlight
anne, a pale white beauty with rosy buttock cheeks,
          slender, self-possessed, smiling
               not the girl he remembers from the bar

she was changed
she took her hand   brushed her hair from her eyes
          rocked to and fro on jim
and sighed

          it was good, she said, to be alive again
          no thought of snow
          of streetlights shining like halos through the snow

but there in the distant sea
a pod of whales each nearly eighty feet in length
made melody and whale song
to jim and anne's lovemaking
the whales cresting piking breaching lobtailing
        their snouts encrusted with callosities
white barnacles here patches of rough skin there
their snouts covered with whale lice
they swam gracefully at slow lumbering velocities
twenty of them
lunging huge and immense in the sea

she rocked on jim making love to him
my flaxen girl, jim said to her, it's good to have you back

you are my flaxen girl
and the night is long

overhead
jet aircraft etched the sky
he watched out the corner of his eye
how their trailings caught the red evening light

the jets etched until the blue vaporous dome
                    parted like a wound
                                leaking red blood

why did they leave home
so young for the trenches

why did they leave home so young
                when the flaxen girl told them: no,

don't go, my hair is flaxen
the night is long, stay home

jim lay in terror watched the sky bleed
                    on anne
                    one drop fell even on him

the white flowers in the field where they lay
were stained with blood
red clouds moved in
massive—ominous—
with pounding hearts
the size of vw buses

the clouds were rent open—a cataract—
red rain came falling out of them
it rained red blood
on anne

until she ran off screaming

ran until she fell near the bowers

ran until she fell and was drowned in it

ran and drowned until she was washed away on a sea of blood

why did they leave home
so young for the trenches . . .

and anne
	she was dead again
	but this time dead for good

jim too was drowning in blood gasping for air
when he was found by a bird watcher
	who stomped the mud in yellow wellingtons
		no stranger to these parts
			he'd been in search of the migrating artic tern
he found instead the convulsing body of jim
near the wreck of his car

he was hauled off by ambulance
                        and there jim saw
                        the white light
                        the lure of it drew him
                        like a fly to a backlit web

he pointed his finger and touched
the sticky matrix of death
like gel it was stuck to him
he withdrew his finger and was at once
pulled back again by the noise
of the screaming siren

later in the hospital
jim said he hated to have been discovered
wished instead he'd been left
                    to have his body turned by the tide
his bones turned and picked clean by the tide
        the tide rolling
        washing jim to sea

where he'd become mere sea debris with anne
        his hands and feet manacled
his body imprisoned by the long bars
                    of sea kelp and seaweed
                    that stretched and wound themselves
downward
and deeper down full fathoms thirty or more
and hooked themselves by the root to the dark sea floor

~~~

recovered from his injuries
jim picked up   drifted
                a new identity is what he sought
                when none arrived heaven-sent
                his father died
                and from his dad he inherited a yacht—
a thirty-eight footer
christened by the old man, the liberty—
he inherited too a small trust to fund it
which if managed correctly would last jim twenty
he moored the sloop at jackson park harbor
                        south side of chicago

here, he wrote a friend,
i can be free, lake waters lapping at my yacht
i'll rename it, the innisfree

and so he sat on his boat
      and reflected on his life
anne dead
his father dead
and then one day
    notified by his brother, chris,
      who chose to send a letter
      instead of phone and tell the truth
that mom
      slowly losing her head
      and control of her bowels
        wanders off
        once almost lost her
        when she escaped our house

        once lost her for three hours at the mall

no other choice
but send her to a home
wish i could do more

wish we
wish i
if only we could do better

barring that
        nothing else to do
                but put her in a home
                and so i've seen to it
                        a decent place
just outside toronto
        i check in from time to time on her
doctors there are experts in alzheimer's

toronto! jim yelled, folding the note
the news struck him like a blow

what did it all mean

>   *it means nothing*
>   *the whole world is a mess*
>   *and from this chaos*
>   *I'm supposed to render sense*

it seemed an unusual punishment to jim
that he must carry on in the wake of terrible tidings like these
and live

>   *not only live*
>   *but I must do something*
>   *make something of this life*

he hadn't amounted to anything yet
so much time   wasted

and now his mother losing her mind
she was only fifty-nine

jim was already twenty-five
not much time left

    surely he should do
something of importance
not just anything would suffice
          many of his childhood friends had gone off to start
            successful careers in banking law medicine
            a few had even formed a rock band
but he   on the other hand
was happy to sit on his yacht, fish, get drunk,
        chat with the birds
        and complain that no clear métier was heaven-sent

occasionally a poem took him by storm
       shook him to the core
       as if his muse had taken a new form:
she now resembled
one who'd been wrecked and killed
     in a car accident
     she invaded him bodily
     took over his soul
     she spoke whole poems into his ear
     they were strange, unsettling, wild-eyed melancholy poems
         he liked to claim after writing them
         that he didn't have a melancholy bone in his body
         it was the muse who was melancholy
                 how else to explain it

     he felt like a tube of skin
     that a snake within him was trying to shed
     but what was odd—
     it was a snake who distinctly was not him:

imagine you are blind
and you come upon me
for the first time
please, touch me
touch my face
as if you were blind
and be filled with the knowledge of who i am

he scribbled the poems as fast as he could remember them
                    that was all the method he brought to it
if he missed it
the poem was gone
as the heat print from a hand
fades from the table when the hand is removed
            is it randall jarrell, he'd mock, laughing at his muse
            or is it a monologue from *spoon river anthology*

it's neither, she said, oh and do you like it?
            have another drink won't you
by the way it's merely a poem to a blind man i once knew

like snow on a petal
your cold words touch me
and my warm feeling for you
goes suddenly chill

the poems were written at all times of day or night
            he scribbled them on any scrap of paper
            thrust them in his pocket
he'd give them to a beggar if only a beggar asked
it was like money from a windfall
 which he would have squandered just as well
            he was careless
a bad steward, he liked to say, of his talent:
i'm just an ass being spoken to by a dead woman

friends urged him to publish his new stuff

            he didn't see what difference it'd make
            if he kept his poetry to himself—what's more
            it's fluff—

that's how he described it
nobody reads poetry

IN THIS DAY AND AGE

OF UBIQUITOUS INFORMATION

WHO READS THIS SHIT ANYWAY

at night after stripping down
he'd pull poems from his pockets
that she'd spoken to him
lay them on his dresser
he'd let them clutter the floors of his cabin
they'd clutter and roll about the floor of his cabin
his cabin would become a floor upon which his poems
would fall
they'd fall upon the floor of his cabin like confetti
such terrible debris
he trod them underfoot
cursed them for getting in the way
rolled them up in balls
who the hell is anne burroughs anyway
he'd pitch them at a makeshift net
hung from his door
and vowed never to publish a single poem again
not as long as she told them to him
never, not ever, nevermore

but there were days he was touched by the beauty of his muse
    loved her voice in his ear
        unlike anything he'd ever known
        at times he vowed he'd do anything to keep her

my future was simple   assured
i came from a good family grew up in the burbs
was one of three sibs: two boys   and me   the girl and
youngest
we wore the following values like a coat of arms:
education and open-mindedness will set you free;
love thy neighbor as you would love thyself—this will give you
peace;
loving thyself will make you happy
and whatever you do, give 110%
that way you won't need to rely on gifts heaven-sent

grew up in my own bedroom
which was painted for the most part lavender
i loved the color lavender
the way certain people love chocolate or a piece of music
for me   lavender was music: a melody that accompanied me
for years my dresser was stuffed with clothes colored
all shades of lavender purple and pink
i wore lavender eye shadow
my junior year in high school i was voted
by a panel of discerning students
        most creative dresser
i decorated my room
            with horses and dolls; seashells and posters of my
favorites:

                sean connery for his masculinity
                shakespeare for his ingenuity
                katharine hepburn for her strong
femininity

                and a picture of buddha for his
serenity

there were other things as well:
collages handmade by me
of things i found while vacationing:
      postcards   abovementioned seashells
      pinecones and needles,
translucent and semi-precious stones
sand of various grits from a dozen beaches
not to mention leaves and acorns
bottle caps   sea-washed glass shards
my favorites cobalt blue   amber and of course phosphorescent
which in a certain light looked lavender

the window of my room overlooked a small field
          where at night   cats would fight
          i'd hear them screech like choking babies
              waking the baying hound down the street
          and he in turn woke the other dogs and more cats
and car alarms would sound
and all things animate and inanimate seemed to bay at the moon

i lived on the attic floor beneath a gable
a skylight had been cut
  so that i lying beneath my sheets
  would be able to fall asleep watching the stars
and moon
  make their slow circuit across the sky
  i learned many constellations by heart
  and which constellations appeared with which
seasons
  venus saturn mars
i could spot them each in their turn
and imagined like some godhead privy to my
  solitary motions
  they could spot me too
  and thus across the distance
  we communicated and talked
  with each other

to venus i told my secretest thoughts
　　　　to mars i must confess　　　　　i sent my worries
　　　　and to saturn i hoped and prayed

i'd fall off dreaming i was out there among them

i describe my room to you so you can know
　　　　that i took good care of myself
　　　　and that jumping in your car to go with you that night
　　　　was something i ordinarily would not have done

i liked you because you seemed
besides handsome
　　　literary and i loved books
　　　　　　there are pictures of me as a very little girl
　　　　　　　　buried under a pile of books
　　　　　　　　hundreds of them

i was read to each night   by both my parents
a routine was early established

> *i'd be tucked in*
> *then read to*
> *then sung to*
> *then prayed for*
> *then kissed good-night*
> *then off with the light*
> > *and hello stars*

i prided myself
on being self-taught
taught myself all sorts of things
how to knit   for instance
and how to type
once built a kite from balsa sticks
*   and wax paper*
flew it into a tree

taught myself from tapes
*   and a book*
*   how to speak spanish*
was learning french the same way
when i met you
i could do all the tenses of to be:
plus-que-parfait
passé-composé
impératif

i taught myself basic car repair
            could replace the plugs
            distributor cap with its wires
            change the oil
            all the filters
i could jimmy a locked door like a thief

i read books on basic   learned
            the language computers speak
            was good at geometry
                    calculus
                    logic
i felt there was something out there
that neither geometry   calculus   nor logic
could capture

i searched until i found the poems
of emily dickinson
i realized while reading her poems
that they were what i had been searching for
all along
i went to college then grad school
      planned to devote my life to her poetry
      planned to raise a hymn to them
and that's when i met you:
though your name was jim
you may as well have gone by fate
            (i read a story or two of fate in my youth
            but fate was always disguised
            as some sort of bogeyman or a skeleton
            with a scythe and clock:
never portrayed as you the man i would meet at the bar
and drive home with on a snowy night innocent enough)

i want you to know that you robbed me of my future
robbed mine (those who knew me or would know me) of me
and me of them
i want you to know
in your bones what you took

i remember standing as a girl
on the muddy bank of a reservoir
i was only ten
staring into the water
> *questioning my reflection*
> *what is it you will be, i asked*
> *what sort of woman shall you be*
> *you are pretty enough*
> *such vague untutored desire and the question:*
> *what will you have given*
> *before you are done?*
i asked it of my reflection
i remember i did

i thought at least i'd have given children
but didn't have a chance to give that

i thought at least i'd have given love
and i did have a chance to give   receive

but now i've lost all that
thought i'd have at least given

my spirit to the world
i imagined even   being old

it seemed only natural i should grow old
avoid mishap—

for mishap happened to others
not to people like me

but i was wrong
for mishap and you

you, jim, you and mishap
the two of you happened to me

after he wrote his poems
        he'd recite them to his friends
        he'd invite them for a party on his yacht
he loved to play the roll of the poet laureate
            it was a public role:
and reading to a public—or group of friends—
connecting a poem to a listener seemed to make poetry whole
            poetry, after all, was an oral art
and quoting it drunk helped him give it all his heart

he stood at the helm of his yacht
a beret or beaver fur cap upon his head
he'd purchased the beret and the cap
from a secondhand shop on clark street
he was invariably dressed in beach motley:
hawaiian shirt, cutoff shorts, thongs on his feet
        he screwed a podium to the deck
            and from behind it declaimed the poems she'd given him
at the side of his podium was a small table
upon which a mounted rabbit
with a worn pelt and antler horns was placed
        this, he said, is what my muse looks like
            he called the jackalope, electra
and sang his songs—or as the case was that summer—
        the poems of anne burroughs

touch me and i bleed from a wound that does not heal
i do not know who i am anymore
i once was a girl who attended swarthmore
straight-a student   soccer team
i yearned as a graduate to be on the faculty
but an accident ended that
so all that remains is this
need for
company
and blood from a wound that doesn't heal

~~~

it was a night—the deck festooned with party lights
friends gathered round the deck the
smell of reefer drifting on the air
     the quiet sound of talk
     from other yachts echoing across the water
     the pulsing lights of jets overhead
tracing their night journeys—
a night the likes of which he'd seldom experienced
there was something in the air
a feeling he'd been here before a sense of his own tininess
               in the scale of things
               his hands felt like empty
balloons
and in each hand he held
a tiny pebble
which he rolled between each finger
            friends of jim's, admirers,
queried
whether he'd deliver a poem that night
people gathered loosely around the podium   and jim

to small applause stepped up to the lectern
removed the beaver cap which sat upon electra
placed it upon his head
clutched the stand with both his hands
noted the deck beneath him swaying
        thought to capture something of this feeling
            was it puniness tininess or the insignificance
            of deed and person
he could not say exactly
when he realized he only felt this way
           to let himself off the hook   he laughed

hardly using his own voice
but speaking as if someone were speaking for him he began:

i took it all and left nothing in return
that is my curse
                    you think it insignificant in the scheme of things
                    but what is insignificant
                    certainly not the things i failed to do

he was silent a while not for lack of anything he had to say
        but because his muse had stilled
        he stood there
        his yacht rocking upon the waves in the harbor
        stood there patiently waiting
        though there were catcalls for more

i hope this isn't the end
　　　　　you've had it you know
you're all washed up, jim
　　　　　　　leave poetry to the poets
　　　　come have some beer

the naked night stalked overhead
and then his own voice recounted what he had seen:

i walked in yellow wellington boots
　　　　　　　hand in hand with a girl named anne
　　　walked through a field of flowers

　　　　　　talking of tomorrow
of orioles in the bowers . . .

they listened to jim
some hooted   some hollered
others said shhh
it was transfixing
     seeing jim up there
         (some thought he was drunk
         others thought he was possessed)
         he stood there in his beaver fur
            reciting his litany as if he were giving voice
            to some inner fire
               or grief
               or emptiness
               which he confessed he didn't know how
               to account for

he opened up his mouth
letting the fire of his words
        consume the night
in fire
in words
he set himself ablaze
jim, inviolate, eyes turned inward
        at the storm breaking within
        was a frenzy of bursting words
those who saw him that night were amazed, appalled
at this wordsmith's self-immolation

it was a castrating performance
a lacerating performance
like a flagellant bracing
for another self-inflicted lashing
        he cursed and cowered
        cursed and cowered

when it was done
his eyes returned   his vision focused
he saw those gathered round stunned
beyond belief
it scared him what he saw
he turned and walked away
          turned and left the stage
he was a virtuoso
a spellbinding performer and this performance

left him charred   hollowed out purified

encore chants from the dazzled crowd were denied
it was the last he performed for an audience
                    after that night   his muse was silence

~~~
some months later
he awoke at the slamming of a door
he realized he wasn't a poet anymore

       easy come
       easy go

i was a bad steward anyway
       but . . . and this is what he told himself
       it's not like i asked for this goddamned role
          not like i asked to be a poet
          not like i asked to be the one who told the world
             what it is
       no   it was never a role i chose

so when the muse quietly left him
he felt disburdened, relieved
     as if he'd just shaken off mortal
responsibility

and the voice that told him do
     when it spoke
now spoke no more
     he was off the hook

he felt glad of it
that's it, he said, good-bye to all that

good-bye, poetry
good-bye, hat

like that

he was free
to come and go

free to stand
at the closing of a door
free to say

i am not like that
            not like that at all

he threw himself a party
it was time to celebrate
           time to maximally inebriate
           and inebriate he did

oh those were the days
           who would have guessed he was such a party
thrower
the parties he threw
     they're legendary now
     no one denies that jim knew how
to throw a party
in his heyday
it didn't matter
if it was monday or payday
     no expense was spared
     he filled his cabin with fine liquor
     called them in two by two

councilmen   aldermen   poets from ireland
doctors   lawyers
sex workers from poland
crooks   cops   what have you
even a judge or two
was wont to show up
dick butkus had even paid a visit
        jim had a picture autographed to prove it
        it was not uncommon to see bill veeck
        studs terkel too bless his soul was a friend of jim's
        or rather a friend of jim's father
        who had been a precinct captain way back in the day
but who's keeping track of who's a friend of whom

all were invited
even friends of little note
        were welcome aboard jim's party boat

for instance there was one hanger-on
a workman named rudy
who hung on and on
              no one quite knows what he did
draft dodger flower child
              he played folk guitar   picked up gigs of sorts
              but his music   nobody could stomach it
              nevertheless   no matter what the weather
jim welcomed rudy
              a rummy is what he was
but as they say
              about birds of a feather they're all cohorts
just bring a friend, jim would exhort, that's all that's needed
a pretty female preferably
preferably with a bob
              (for that's how jim liked them—hair cut short above
              the shoulders)
      but if you must come alone, uninvited
      please note: it's strictly byob

actually jim was quite disinterested in women
     fucking them that is
     anne cured him of that
     but that's not the way jim tells it
to anyone who will pull up a stool and listen
he tells it with a sigh
     to get his fill, he'd say,
     he'd do three a day
it didn't matter how he got it
     just as long as he didn't get nil
     and if he did strike out
the way he'd sulk
     swear cuss the moon

he'd throw a girl overboard who turned him down

he swore by straight talk
didn't like fuss

approach a woman, he'd council,
    tell her what you want
    be direct: don't be afraid to touch
    you might be surprised at the results

once in a while if he had to
he'd take one forcibly
    hold her mouth in case she screamed

    he describes walking the deck at his parties
    predatory

he estimates he did forty girls in a single year
many of them in the lavatory

it's all lies of course—anyone will tell you—
or big talk or faulty memory

or legend building which was something he did years later at
the bar
his cronies gathered round confusing anecdote with testimony

in reality he fell in love with one
a raven-haired beauty named mae fairweather
—it makes him sigh to think of her—
           she was fey delicate
had a forgetful way about her
as if she'd spent too much time getting high
but she didn't smoke
hardly touched a drink
her attitude was meant to disarm, make people think
        she was something other
        than what she was and what she was was
this: a blue-blooded girl who
            beneath her flaky exterior had
grace   nerves of steel
she was also quite self-possessed
she could do with jim   or without him
                        it was all the same to her
            so   well she gave herself him
                  those three summer months
                  then took herself away

(by the way, the things mae and jim did during those three months would take a novel to express, especially if we were to take into account jim's complex and messy emotions for mae: she was his lover mother sister daughter enemy and brother

she was his own best critic she despised his poetry which pleased jim to no end if, on the other hand, we were only to take into account mae's emotions for jim a brief grocery list might suffice: he happened to be available was modestly capable she was bored what's more she always wanted to spend the summer on a boat let us just say they spent the majority of that summer in the hay jim couldn't get enough of mae what's more it astonished him that he'd discovered someone so beautiful so lighthearted so blue-blooded so ready and steady and levelheaded she on the other hand could barely stomach jim he was a drunkard for chrissakes! she'd mock him call him fool she thought he was disgusting really she barely tolerated his friends she despised all the parties he threw she never did understand why he did it: throw the parties that is, he tried to explain said it was de rigueur, fun but she didn't understand the sense of serving all of those drunken cronies free especially when it was obvious they preferred the booze to jim's company of all the friends that she met, rudy was the worst of them she nicknamed him the peeping tom she swore he was going to be the end of them more than once she caught him spying on her peering through the porthole at her and jim in addition she was the kind of girl who

while making love   loved to sigh and moan in bed she
gave no thought to controlling it yet her sighing and moaning
seemed a siren call to rudy who couldn't resist her strenuous
tones of bliss she once or twice chased him—and she half-na-
ked—around the deck with broom in hand then she'd scream
at jim and demand he get rid of him or "i'll be gone" which was
a threat unfortunately for jim
he didn't take seriously but she showed him)

just like that   a snap
of the fingers poof she was gone

her sudden   departure
broke   jim   down

drove him nuts
cleaved him with regrets
one moment she was here next minute gone
the memory of her body (her sweet lithe supine body!)
was still warm in his hands
yet she was gone
        gone
                gone
                        on to other men
or other women as the case may be
or even on to celibacy
which from time to time was her wont

but he wanted more of mae   longed for her
which brings us to the general question

why did she leave him
        though there are no real answers
        yet she'd have vouched she was bored with him
bored with his liquor   his belligerence
his judgment in friends
all of which seemed at first temporary qualities
but proved to be permanent

he, on the other hand, thought everything was perfect
she must have found out about his accident with anne
how else explain it
it must have made her sick, he figured, that's why she split

yet if she should come back (he held out hope)
      —she arriving in linen white
      her hair done up and haloed against the light
      of the setting sun—
he swore he'd do anything to keep her
give up poetry give up drink sell the boat get a job buy a house
in the suburbs if necessary
but if she should stay away indefinitely
he'd do just about anything to end the pain
      get doused in gasoline send himself up in flames

      it was the bomb never falling that fell on jim
      love requited was now love gone wrong
      the loss of mae smote his heart like a beaten drum

he almost killed himself in the wake of her departure
gave himself over to unholy drinking
    mostly gin sometimes whiskey
    practiced risky behavior
    played russian roulette   with a gun
    once while drunk he thought it'd be cool
        to challenge someone to a duel
        it was a dispute over money
        or over who insulted whom
someone called mae a whore or perhaps a bitch
a whore, jim said, let's shoot it out
they were acting like idiots
faced off in an alley
standard fifteen paces jim turned shot prematurely
(mae wasn't surprised when she heard of this)
almost killed his opponent
but worse he almost had his head blown off
for breaking the rules—jim was never one for rules—
and carted away in a hearse

when friends caught wind of jim's behavior
they counseled him to stay calm
  even his brother chris who'd rescued him in the past
  was called upon to do his best
  he flew in from ontario
    where he ran a small concern
    manufacturing stereos
he showed up on jim's yacht
tried to talk sensibly with him
but jim didn't care
  where chris came from
  nor what concern he ran
he was wild with grief
without mae what was the point of being here

the point, said chris, is that we need you

who can say why but jim thought chris disingenuous
and told him it wasn't any of his business
go home, he told chris, back to where you came from
you always had it better than me
what's more you've always been condescending

it was the talk of a drunk for jim had been drinking
        and chris left—flew out of town thinking—
        it was the last he'd see of his brother jim

fights one end of town to the other ensued
it was a disgrace to see him now
his face covered with cuts and bruises

his thumb was broken
but it didn't matter so long as his heart was broken too

he was determined to have mae back
and that's all he seemed to want to do

he haunted bars where she was wont to go
the rainbo club in particular (on damen street)

was a haunt of hers why she liked it he didn't know
it was a damned ridiculous place made him sick

he felt out of his element when he stepped into the place
the door slammed behind him like a statement

he found himself surrounded by
yuppies hipster wannabes harlequins
pretentious folk
a bunch of strange exotic fish
at the bottom of the sea is what they seemed
they seemed to communicate
not by speech
but by fashion and facial expression

find someone among them who was essential to the core
(as jim was, for instance)
such a task would have proved not merely impossible
but what for?

when i was a boy i used to see
the sea-fish swim at the aquarium
(the deep-sea fish exhibit is the one for me)
coelenterate, ratfishes, chimaera, batfishes, frogfishes, sea toads,
the black swallower,
the lanternfish with its luminous head and body are just
some of the fishes that i adore

now i'm a man and in lieu of the aquarium
i go instead to the rainbo club
(a fashionable bar on damen street)
> *i'm struck by how like deep-sea fishes*
> *the late-night fashionable folk*
> *at the rainbo club are*

you have the black swallower   for instance
a fellow who stands by the bar in
fashionable clothes and throws shots
of hard liquor down his throat
as if it were coal into a furnace
and like coal it fuels his engine of loquacity
he speaks of nothing so offhandedly
as his unquenchable appetite
for material things:
fast cars—faster women—
he thinks he'd like to take you too
watch him close: he'll consume you
        whole
        just like that—one bite!
        then mop his mouth clean with his tie

you'll also spy the lantern fishes:
they come in all sizes
though usually they're small and slight
and drift in swimmingly after midnight
how they shine as if lit
from an interior light:
how they shimmer near the edge
         of something dark and precipitous
they are females mostly
in skimpy dress
with large eye-goggle eyes
beaming smiles   that'll stop your heart
         they sit luminous animate and ghostly
         in small groups and light
         the darkest corner of the bar

friends of mae's who frequented the bar called her
let her know
that this madman
her old beau
lay there in wait asking for her
    she didn't doubt it
    it put her in a rage
    the little man is after me, she said,
    she knew from the first
    he was no good—a bad apple—
    an unseemly beast let loose from the cage
    to rant and rave through town—
    why didn't he just do every one a favor
    leap off his yacht and drown
    bring rudy the peeping tom with him   while he was at it
    but jim had other plans   he wanted to be her savior

one night in particular
he was at the rainbo club
rudy was by his side but ditched jim by nine
(since jim was on this mission to reclaim mae
    it was impossible to say boo to him
        without him threatening to break your leg)
so that night, good and soused,
        wounded wasted and wondering
when mae would step through the door
he pushed a bartender up against the wall
(whom, he thought, might have been a friend of mae's)
nose to nose he held him there against the wall
tell me, he screamed, where is she, where is my mae

i don't know swore the bartender
jim thought he was gay
called the bartender faggot
tell me, faggot, where is she
i can't say, said the bartender
a fight ensued
with disastrous results for jim

three bartenders came to the first one's aid
pinned jim down
      each one taking aim
the offended bartender
      kicked jim clean in the kidney
showed no mercy
gave jim a menacing clout on the temple

it was enough to knock jim out
they grabbed him   the four of them
hauled him by his hair through the bar hectored him
sat him up in a chair saw his turtle scar laughed at his
        turtle scar
          slapped him
            mocked him   called him clown
    dragged him into the alley
    stood him up knocked him down
    left him there for rats or bugs or cops   or thugs or
death

jim lay there crumpled his head in a pool of blood
    rats
        chewed his ear
    perhaps he was dead
        or half alive and pitched near death

if only he could slide off the rack into the abyss
because if he were dead it'd be fine with him
he was tired of life
he lay there in the alley
there was no white light

        just nausea pain and delirium

at three a.m. he pulled himself up
        found a sink in a gas station washed himself off
          took a public bus home
it rumbled down desolate city streets
    paper and debris drifted on the hot summer air
        the hot air bore it all away
            bore another day's trash into the hot evening
sky

jim's head rumbled too
        his thoughts drifting here and there
        occasionally the driver checked jim out in the rearview
mirror
he heard jim talking:
i'll go back there kill all three of them i will
        stand them up against the wall and mow them down
        they make fun of me they'll see what'll come to them

hey, the driver asked, if you don't mind me saying you look a
wreck

yeah, i got in a fight over a girl it's not worth fighting for
but if events were to play themselves over
i'd get in the same fight again
        i suppose that's the way i am
        i can't explain it
no regrets no looking back but forward forward into the fire
i've half a mind to catch a bus going in the opposite direction
        take me back there
if you think i'm kidding let me tell you i'd give them a scare

but what the hell
they don't know what i'm going through
        i lost my girl just want her back
                frankly, they have nothing at all to do with that

jim was quiet
the bus driver spoke up:
                tell me where you need to go
                i'll take you there

just take me home, jim said, thanks
                i live on a yacht at jackson park harbor
                        for three years it's been my home
                        it sucks to live on land
                        it sucks to live on water
                        had i a choice to do it over
i'd choose to be an albatross
                and live alone on air

she was my mayflower queen all the way
        my mae

terse with direct statement
        that was the way with my mae

bring me flowers in spring:
                lilac hyacinth lilies
                at my dying remember i had a flare for living

                wool for spinning sweaters of the finest angora
                        skirts spun from silk

        tennis court at nine a.m.
                        at noon, tea

        earl gray
                a touch of sugar cream
        in gold painted china of the most delicate sort
                such was the way of my mae

rare pearls dangled her ears
a three carat diamond in a ring
toes to tickle on a sun-dappled afternoon while drinking
champagne
          (we drank a hell of a lot of champagne)

               but a foul mouth she had
               a temper only this side of raging
               she'd cut you to pieces

i loved my mae was wasted on her
loved her the moment her eyes disposed of me
          mocked me made me feel small

it was her strength
pitted against my weakness

i knew from the first it was mae's way or the highway
she treated me like garbage   nearly killed me she did
i wished she had
i never had it better

the bus driver laughed:
>sounds like she's a tough case
>i had a wife like that
>the way she could cut me down to size
>her eyes smoldering she barely saying a word
>i loved her too couldn't get enough of her
>>but she left me just like that
>>>married a dentist
>had two kids moved to the burbs
>>>glencoe as a matter of fact
my advice to you:
do whatever you must
>>but get over it soon as you can
>>and remember shit happens
even to the best of us

jim listened to the bus driver nodded off
while the bus bumped through town
he slept a while   and while he slept
he had a vision of a whale stirring the water   with its
tail

~~~

years went by
slowly he weaned himself of mae
he tried to clean up his act
but failed   ended up selling his yacht

          . :
         .   :
      . . . . .   :
             :
             :

(a car had been driven off the dock
        and landed on its deck destroying all
              but the hull)

$3,200 in bills was what he got
which was fine for a boat that no longer sailed
a drinking binge left him broke
he drifted in and out of neighborhoods
        stayed a few months in an uptown s.r.o.
        then drifted back to hyde park
        settled in a furnished studio
        walking distance from a bar that was to become
except for a few months reprieve his last destination

he sat in his plain bare room
      unfolded a sheet of paper
        licked the tip of his pen
began his epic poem:

at three in the afternoon
planes crisscrossing overhead

leaving o'hare airport and heading east
for new york city or god knows where

on one of the hottest days of the dog-day summer
with heat-stricken people

collecting in lines behind the bubblers
drawing water into parched throats

or into empty plastic bottles pouring it
onto heads shoulders necks and backs

and heat-fatigued runners
panting pounding. . . .

the epic would be something he wrote
to confirm his stay on earth
      it would be something composed in the grand style
            he'd take his time with it
   no hurry
   a project to last a lifetime
that's the way he conceived of it
he began but it sat for months   maybe years untouched
he became a bartender
an after-hours drunk always the life of the party
but a poet too—so he adopted the look:
   wild-eyed shaggy uncouth uncombed
breath that reeked of tobacco and booze
     he was a drunk undone
when asked by old friends
who remembered him in his glory years on the yacht
what he was up to
   he told them he wasn't slipping just hanging out
working on   his poem: an epic

he'd tell them that this poem was going to confirm
his stay on earth
he was made for doing such a work
it'd be a word of warning
possibly a political statement who could say
but one thing is for sure:
it'd be a tract railing against the state of things
for he was always railing against the state of things—
how things had changed   for the worse
how people coming up these days lacked values
that he'd known as a youth
every one corrupted by a permissive culture
every one indulging their own idiosyncratic whims
       because that's what they were told to do
exploit their idiosyncrasies for fame
                 eternal renown   dough
       he railed that if things didn't change soon
       the shit would hit the fan—literally—

there'd be an uprising   a mutiny
the little guy heaving his cutlass in the salt marsh
each and every soul would march against the man in all his
guises
the man being a trickster who posed
as politico-advertising-guru-spin-meister-impresario
a chameleon who courted fools with sex fame and fortune
but when it came time to deliver the goods he came up short
he was a chameleon therefore who should and would
be struck down once and for all: dead
whereupon a return would be forged to universal morals
        agreed upon by an authority akin to the church
and a sense of man's puniness would be restored—
which he argued had been lost on the day
the stars had been blotted out by luminous urban streetlight

but man's puniness   his fundamental insignificance
were the grand themes of his poem
when completed it would be a masterpiece
he wouldn't make it public unless it proved
            an epic beyond compare   trust me, he would say
                        i've had poems published in years past
you know i was once well known in the journals
                        recently i told a noted publisher
who wanted the rights to my out-of-print collection
that i've burned it all   burnt it all in an inferno
compared to this epic everything else i've written—
all my poems—are minor   not worth my name
                        but this work, my epic, i'm made for it
and when completed it will win me posthumous fame

sometimes they or graduate students would ask him about
        "the poem"
        can i see it, they'd ask
                still working on it, he'd say
not ripe yet
                when it's done you'll see
it concerns a whale
no it's not moby dick
this poem is about my whale
                a sperm, he joked

then he'd tell them about his out-of-body experience
        that he experienced in his car wreck with anne
        how he approached the light and was told
        to do
        this epic is my doing, he said: my reckoning

jim jotted notes from time to time
        when no one was looking
        but that was that
        he never seemed to be in the right frame of mind
        perhaps his muse had escaped
        if so how to get it back
he tried to remember
        eyes turned back summoning her to song
he turned his eyes back sober
he turned them back drunk
but still not a line
        still not a song

when pressed he quoted what he could remember
        of an older time:

i'm preyed upon by things:
bad dreams, a penchant for lying, mendacity,
i walk a turtle waddle live
        beneath a shell
pass a bottle around
like a turtle i'll come tumbling down

it was all an act
     appreciated by amateur connoisseurs
     of the spoken art
they came from near and far
loved jim for it
     he was such a character
the tavern's bard
     quick with a quip
he had become a barkeep a drunk
who claimed to be writing an epic

and the claim was all he had to show for it
the claim   a few scraps of paper   a drink
but his muse—whom he had relied on for years—was silent
his once fresh talent had become empty and derelict

PART II

~~~

sing to me muse   a song
                   of the long-haired woman

shall we call her gretchen or june
       or june or gretch
       she works all day long
       her hair tied up in a bun
       her hair wrapped and tied in a net
       her hair tucked neat beneath a net in a bun
       her name: gretchen or june
               or june or gretch

she works all day long in the greek diner on the corner
       is she loveless forlorn as she seems
serving meals to customers like you and me

standing outside at break she smokes a virginia slim
    one foot propped against the red-brick wall
    one foot in the grave
    she says she never smokes never sins
        votes democratic drinks gin thinned with tonic
        she itches the instep of her foot and sneezes

        gretchen or june or june or gretch
        she serves greek meals which she detests
        she's a vegetarian
        once was valedictorian
        once nearly prom queen

once a champ on the swim team
long distance was her metier
        she was voted most likely to succeed
        but now she thinks she hasn't
            succeeded
                of course

she loved horses till about the age of ten
and until ten she owned a steed
when she fell and broke her pelvis
       that was that
             it cured her of her horses
                     now she waits for the day to end

waits watching the clock

waits watching the hour hand make its slow circuit round the dial

waits watching the long dull day drain away

all orders in
                  all orders out
                              it makes her want to shout

is she loveless and forlorn as she seems
serving meals to customers like you and me

has her life
melted into a blob of dull days

have the years
of her life
become
a dull blob

should she have cut her hair short and bought a fob
        for a gorgeous lovely man, ricardo,
                she knew him years ago
                        he played the mandolin
                                spoke chinese dealt antiques
                everything was strictly mandarin
                        18th 19th were the centuries he collected
                                he was quite a specialist

        he asked if she would come with him
                no time limit specified
                indefinite
                unending

        to a town outside beijing
        all expenses paid

    but it was a proposal
        without a ring

she said, reluctantly, i can't go ricardo, i have this job
you're kidding, he said
she said, no, i'm not kidding at all

one day he up and left her
never returned to see her
        never a note   not a card never a call
        she often wondered what became of him
        often she second-guessed herself
        —should i have picked up gone
        with him—

                        to beijing without a ring

she questioned her memory
he wasn't even a film that she might pop into her video
he wasn't even the sound of a voice
on a tape that she might play on her cassette
he wasn't even a picture for no pictures were taken
he wasn't even handwriting for no letters were written
impossible to believe he existed at all

true she loved him playing the mandolin
loved him deep inside of her
she loved him from the heart of him
to the outermost reaches of his outermost
skin

was he flesh and muscle
skin and bone alone
        or something else entirely
        he seemed unreal   at times ethereal

sure he could be metaphysical transcendental he dabbled in
judo
        studied philosophy—strictly continental—
        ate tons of french vanilla ice cream
was devoted to the virgin mary

        but what did all this make him
    she did not know
        nor could she say
        it was simply a resumé really
           not the man
    if she could
        perhaps she'd say ricardo was like

rain in october

falling
      on
          bare
               branches

but who would believe her

    and if she said she loved him
    because she hated him
    because he didn't take a stance
    on the two of them as a couple   who could doubt her

once or twice since he left she heard it
in a café or at a movie once over the radio
the sound of the mandolin played pizzicato
it helped her memory make him real again
ricardo, she says, and says it again: ricardo in the rain,
but it was o so long ago
           so long
               she just doesn't know
ricardo

she waits watching
    the clock
    one foot against the wall
        one in the grave
        smokes another

how many times must the slow arm go round the dial:

eight or nine or ten
        before
        she can say
        i am free to go and come as i please
        free to feel the heat against my skin

            free to face the elements
            nude or clothed
            semi-nude semi-clothed

she did that once in a st patrick's day parade
                    sat on a float
              wrapped in a leaf
          propped atop a castle
there was even a moat

semi-clothed thus with leaf it began to downpour
                 off with leaf
it seemed so simple

                rain—nude

                it caused an uproar

nude and wet in the rain
the smell of pavement in the rain
the taste of metallic rain on her tongue
the smell of tar and lilacs in the rain
it made her laugh the feel of it
the freedom of it
the sight of it
atop a float for all to see

nude—rain

the smell of dumpster trash and grease in the heat
her foot kicked up against the wall
the smell of trash in the heat the stifling smell
of trash in the heat the sound
of raccoons and rats rummaging in the dumpster in the heat
in the night
of shouts in the alley of car alarms on the street
of fire alarms in the distance
of streetlights flickering on
and night descending

free to step out
into a fresh spring rain
free to be the person
who she is
who she was
who she will be mandolin or no
the person inside her who never changing always is

free to say:
this is who i am stepping
into a fresh spring rain
the rain falling down
the light rain wetting my face

the cool refreshing rain running down my face my tongue gut-
tering the cool metallic rain the rain falling wetting my hair the
fresh rain wetting my brows my lashes the rain falling collecting in my palms my feet splashing in the rain-soaked streets
the streets made slick with rain the rain splashing in the gut-
ters the downspouts flooded with rain the green sod sodden
with rain the cars and buses splashing by in the rain the mud
puddles over-spilling with rain the rain-chased worms fleeing
the loamy earth and she saying:

this is me
this is who i am
   i am geraniums in the spring rain
    i am red and pink geraniums
in the spring rain
   i am geraniums on the back porch
i am a blooming flower in the spring rain
i am roots into the wet damp earth
   i am one with the elements
i am not the blob of all my days
   melted into a blob of days
   i am rainwater falling and not rainwater falling

all orders in   all orders out
   it makes her want to shout

~~~

she loved another completely unlike mr ricardo
  it frightened her that she would love
two so antipodal

  it came to be the one she loved
—was jim—
in his post-poet phase
the drunk who looked the poet but couldn't write a single
phrase

she had worked at the diner eight years
       since ricardo left her
       and since ricardo left
she lived a regular patterned life
           based on a schedule that seldom varied
           others were always in a fit of strife
           but she with her schedule was seldom harried
           one night when her t.v. broke down
           and the a.c. in her building went kaput
           she shut her apartment door behind her
took a walk up the street to the bar
           and there she discovered its bard
           to her surprise she liked him
it was the attention paid her in a moment
that did it
he cleared a seat   told her sit
something in her yearned for company and comfort
and this cozy place and his pleasant smile were it

jim liked her ways
she seemed simpler than mae
        safer than anne
she was a woman with intelligence—he could see that—
a touch of elegance
it was also clear she had suffered
     and because she suffered she might
find a way to understand him

at first the routine between them seemed simple
pure
              he was a drunk   for sure
              but she might be his cure
what would be the harm in trying
she sidled up to him at the bar a few times a week or so

soon it was habit
then home to his place too drunk to say no

she was told: beware   watch out
he's a touch violent
sulky
prone to be insolent
     can be crafty
dangerous difficult

       what's more he tells lies
        in friendship he can't be trusted
he's full of bitterness   blame   duplicity

    she thought she could outsmart him
        in truth he sometimes seemed slightly dim
        not as quick as she
           but that was part of his craft, she was told,
          —watch out—
     his slowness   for sure   had a certain charm

especially
    when he was trying
       to remember something
          he couldn't put his finger on
then he'd make it up   he could be quite a cut-up
once in a while he'd quote her a poem
but not often
he was tired of playing that role
tired of being a bard: it had reduced him to a joke
he was looking for a new role   one that would let him
be entirely jim   whatever that was

once in a while
        they'd rent a room at a motel
        there was one in chinatown they liked called the beijing
        nude prints and chinese characters on the wall
        the place was otherwise a dump
        but it was home away from home a sort of
camp:
bed   dresser with drawers
        a small fridge for alcohol
        beige drapes made of vinyl

        the prints on the wall put her in mind of ricardo
whatever happened to ricardo
        to mr ricardo of october rain
she wondered as jim plundered her

there was the zanzibar too of course
                              vibrating beds
                              porno on the tube
                              she didn't care for it
                                    the fake flesh of it
                                    the close up diagnostic
                                    shots of it
                                    the fake sighs
the fake moans
the fake orgasms
the fake everything
fake   fake   fake
for   a   buck
                              but jim liked it
                                    without it he couldn't get it up
                                          but with it he was a genie
unloosed from his jar at the zanzibar
you have three wishes   my dear
i'll fulfill each   in its turn . . .

back then it was sex that bound them
no-holds-barred sex
based on total honesty
        mutual chemistry
        drunken accord and a bit of levity
                she told him exactly what she desired
                        she was blunt with him
oral   anal
no first lick it
then prick it
now lick it more
he gave it to her then some

                        in the heat of passion
he slapped her called her whore
it became a regular thing
                        but it was the only time he'd slap her
                        in the heat of fucking

she once told a friend about it
beware he'll give you a scare
he urinates on me too
beware he'll give you more than a scare

but it's fucking, gretchen said, it's fine fucking fucking

when they woke up—sometime later next morning—
        they popped a bottle of champagne in celebration
        it was always a celebration to be with jim
        life of the party once again
        morning noon and night—here's to you, girl, he'd toast
        hair of the dog that bit you
        cheers

sometimes he'd show up to the diner half drunk
watch her work
    he said she had some moves
    she had a figure to match
    she knew just how to wear her clothes
    he once brought her long-stemmed roses in a gift-
wrapped box
    once brought her
brand new shoes
    with half-inch insoles
    he swore arch support was the key
    to everything including luck   and happiness
cheers, he said, when she unwrapped the box and kissed him

if a customer got short with her
he'd wait outside cuss him
get rough

once threw a guy against the wall
don't come back i'll kill you i will

what's more he was never happy with the tips she got
twenty percent wasn't good enough
at the end of the night he liked to collect his bit
he'd take her tips cash and change count it up then split it
sixty forty he reasoned
after all she kept her hourly pay
she agreed to it, what the heck, she spent more than half her time
at his place

at the bar
       jim got along with every one
       he was a regular guy
       one of the people
       generous with his time
       never forgot a name or a face always quick with a line
       he was once handsome but now drink was ruining him
       (a tooth or two had rotted out and he suffered from gout)
nevertheless
he had a certain grace
it made you watch him
it was physical   beautiful

one person though   thought jim a fake
it was the tavern's cook
whom no one paid   any attention to
her name was francine   she wore a wig slightly askew
was missing all but five teeth
three of which were capped with gold
she was black   american
old as the oklahoma hills where she was born
she was a palmist filled with strange superstitions
oh the stories she could tell
of sea creatures and monsters
she had known as a girl in oklahoma
and there was this little red man with pointed horns
        who chased her round a field of corn
when you pointed out
there were no sea creatures in oklahoma
much less corn
she would scream: what are you talking about
don't you tell me

francine never read a book on psychology
yet she could divine a person's soul with just one look
    it was uncanny
some thought it voodoo
others thought it hindu
which was crazy, really,
    for it was merely physiology
    the eyes the window to the soul
    she had a knack for it
        no denying that

gaze into the tunnels of my eyes and be lost
    in a windblown world of breaking hopes
    and a shipwrecked country
    of green-blue dreams. . . .

she was expert at the penetrating look
it only took a second to chase it out of its nook
        but the shape of the soul was divined
francine took one look at jim
knew all there was to know of him
she didn't like the sight of it
her diagnosis and this didn't require magic:
he was corrupt   mean to the core
          a lousy drunk a bore what's more
          he'd probably die of cirrhosis
her prognosis: steer clear
there's no hope, dear, if you stay with him
          he's ruining you
          please listen to me
          you shouldn't be in here anyway
drinking your money away
a beautiful girl like you
          you could have a good man any day
      why do you choose jim

she tried to explain it to francine but couldn't

   look into my eyes, francie, and tell me why i can't explain

i'm a fool for love, i suppose, what else to report

you're a fool all right, was francine's retort

but francine paused looked into gretchen's eyes
saw something in her soul
      no doubt about it
            it gave francine a chill

girl, she said, the sea creatures i have known
      you shall know far worse than i
      such a tender girl   i fear for you

then be my protector, francie, and look after me   please

there were times however
        when francine's
dire prognostications
seemed a miscalculation
        when all was clear justification
she swore she'd never forget
            how jim and she would fish
            for perch or bass or bream
                in the south shore harbor at the
                south shore yacht club
                the sailboats in the harbor
                he knew them all by heart

his heart was in a sailboat, he told her,
that sailed in the sea of his mind
he told her that the sea that fills his mind
is a sea of brandy on wednesdays a sea of
whiskey
on thursdays and on fridays a sea of gin
which touches greener shores
than any known by man
he'd like to sail her there
someday
by god it'd be fun, he'd say

he could be such a sot

sometimes he talked a bunch of rot:
he was full of lake lore
that would make her laugh

there's a whale in this lake, he'd tell her
no there's not

yes   a humpback   probably   though maybe a blue
            massive   large as a ship
            with frightful porthole eyes
            it swims the sea of lake michigan
            has been reported in parts of lake huron
            once spotted
as far north as whitefish bay
no one knows
how it
            got to the great lakes
            perhaps the saint lawrence seaway

no one knows
how it's survived this long in lake water

perhaps it's a new freshwater species undiscovered if not
it should have been beached
                    perished of sickness
                    but instead it persists

is it a whale or something else entirely
like the monster of loch ness
                    only a few have actually seen it
                    it's hardly been reported
i myself have seen the monster

once during a storm
on my yacht
making my way to mackinac
i was caught in a squall
the wind kicked up
i was whipped by wind
                    slashed by rain
                    overcome by eight-foot waves

i was hanging by the wires
scudding through a trough
nearly washed in

     when the whale emerged brushing the side of my boat
         i reached out touched its fin
         it blew
         i nearly fell in
         but   hung on
         its huge jaws opened wide
             its eye horrible
             its teeth its tongue
i saw down its throat
like jonah
it wanted me i know
for a meal
but instead water from an eight-foot wave sluiced in and it was
gone

gretchen sat there rapt
while he talked his rot the sun set
impossible that someone she knows
should be spinning sea yarns
she laughed at the thought of it
impossible that her man jim
should swear by a whale in the lake

        it gave her strange comfort
        to be near him
        she felt free from harm
        he was a force elemental
he wrapped her in his arm
        was drunk on brandy grew sentimental
        come here, my dear
        promise me one thing
don't leave me
believe me   i couldn't go on without you

just then he felt his genie rise from its jar
you have three wishes, my dear
i'll fulfill each
in its turn

          you only need specify

          and specify she did

          at that jim's pole jerked once twice
          he yanked up

lo
and reeled in a fish
they hopped in his car
     drove home to his place
     blind pie-eyed drunk laughing

~~~

      he quoted her a poem
his eyes turned back
      and with his eyes turned back
      he remembered a bit of the old feeling
      and with a bit of the old feeling
he let what had built up inside of him
spill out of the jar like a genie

it wasn't supposed to happen like this
i tell you because i'm drunk and hell
    we've been together a while
    and there's some things you should know about me
    i tried to do the best with what i had
    but i failed miserably
    the thing is when i started out
        i mean at the beginning of this thing
        i had the best of intentions
        i knew i had a gift
        i just didn't know what the shape
            of my gift was
        and if you have a gift, the chinese fortune says,
            give to it your fullest
            or let it destroy you

to hell with chinese fortunes
    i never saw one i thought would come true

        anyway i attempted to give my gift
        which was poetry

        but my gift wasn't so easily given

        WHO READS THIS SHIT ANYWAYS
        AND WHAT THE HELL IS THE POINT

let me put that another way
i was one of five: second and the problem child
jealousy and selfishness were bred into me
i did what i needed to do to survive

what i'm saying is i wasn't necessarily a very easy giver
sure with the booze
                    i'd let the tap flow for any and all
                    but you see that was selfish too
                            i had an image to promote
                            not to mention for years
                            i lived with a phobia
                            about drinking alone
but that—that phobia—it's long since been   blasted out by
the root
                    i'd sooner drink now than anything else
                    if i could give up sleep i would
                    if i could spend more time drunk
                                        i would
                    and i'd do it alone or in a crowd
                    it no longer matters

            but going back a little
when it came time to give what i should give
                    when it came time to put the heave-ho
                    into my end of the deal
i mean we were each put on the planet for a purpose
i failed miserably

i cannot tell you exactly how that failure happened
how it was exactly i gave up poetry
      whether it was a car accident
      and its aftermath that slowly drained it out of me
      or a certain lifestyle i chose to live
      you know
interestingly i idolized a drunken poet
        before i had even gotten drunk or had written a poem
        it was with infinite wisdom
        i decided to emulate dylan thomas
        you think it's stupid
            i agree
        for in retrospect i don't give a damn about his poetry
        o sure do not go gentle into that dark night
            but rage rage rage
        i liked that one   and i liked a line here or there
          like: twisting on the racks till their sinews give way
        but in general he and i were two different fishes
it was his lifestyle   see   that attracted me
i was hooked on it and i wasn't even thirteen
        now i ask: why didn't i want to be a lawyer
            doctor teacher something respectable
            why was i stuck on being a fucking
            poet
            why a drunk
            o i could go on

      WHO READS THIS SHIT ANYWAYS
      AND WHAT THE HELL IS THE POINT

i could spread the blame i could lay it thick
but i'm looking right now for causes in me
because i think it matters
right now that i'm forthright with this

when it was time to fork left with the rest of the pack
get on with my life: find a wife a house
move to the burbs get a job
i forked right i wanted to go it alone
the damned stubbornness that has plagued me   ·
plagued me then
i wanted to   carve my own track
                   trace my own destiny against the stars
                   i chose poetry and set up shop on a yacht

the poems i was making
even early on
they came out of me
        at all times of day or night
                it was like a torrent
                hell i couldn't write fast enough to keep up
                        i don't know where they came from
                        or how
                        they just appeared like that
                        never a problem to produce a poem
                        i was born for it
                        here i'll show you how i did it
                        look at my eyes and watch
                        i turn them back like this:

gaze into the tunnels of my eyes and be lost
        in a windblown world of breaking hopes
        and a shipwrecked country
        of green-blue dreams. . . .

it all happened so easily
so readily
they came so steadily
it's hard to explain what happens
                    water water everywhere and not a drop to drink
                    i didn't see the urgency to do anything with it
                    instead of taking my gift seriously
                    i turned it into a party trick
and then i turned into the party
i was selfish i suppose you could say
                    or i was scared of failure
                    or i didn't have what it took to do it right
but i'm getting ahead of myself and laying blame
look i had what it took
                    i wrote a silly poem about a turtle
                    when i was sixteen   it was a national
sensation
i wrote more poems
and everything i wrote
                    found its way into the journals
                    they said i was an american rimbaud
                    mentors older than verlaine
were knocking at my door
they came smooth-talked me like suitors
                    there was a collection
                    rave notices

                    WHO READS THIS SHIT ANYWAYS
                    AND WHAT THE HELL IS THE POINT

but at that point i was too drunk to care
people tried to shake me out of it
my own brother chris tried to shake me out of it
not to mention the mentors
they were fascinated by my trick
and when they saw me do it
they realized they had something here
they took me to poetry fairs
exhorted me to turn my eyes back & etc. & etc.
they wrote my poems down for me
carted them away had them published
i insulted one and then another
i even insulted my brother
there's a limit to what people will take
especially when it comes to a poet
    who claims to be doing it for art's sake

there's other things you should know
things that make my heart sick
very few people who know me now
know about a night that i never forget
i was in the full flush of my talent
    and being very careless
    drinking every night in the bars
when a woman—i think a graduate student—
stepped up to the bar
she knew something about my talent
she sought me out because of it
hey, she said to me, aren't you that poet
who does that thing with your eyes
it irritated me that i was known as the poet with an eye problem

so i thought what the hell
may as well take advantage of it
milk it   you see   for all it was worth
i figured out what she was looking for
she wanted

                the authentic
                the angry
                the gifted
                the broken

                        poet

she didn't want art

                so i gave her
                what she wanted

                played siegfried sassoon or something like that
                and became an actor with a part

it wasn't so innocent you see

i was tired of poetry   of the unbearable pain
of veracity

i found mocking the role of poet came easily
what's more i wanted something in return
         i demanded it
         you want your performer
your performance
         fine you got it
         but now you must do something for me
         so we got up from the bar
she did a drunken little dance
i hooked my arm around her and slipped my finger
between her skin and pants

      i shouldn't have been driving that night
         but the risk was part of it
             part of what
             she wanted

         drove off in a snowstorm
         trying to get her home to my place and bed
         fast as possible
         when i smashed into the back of a plow
         and killed her   she smashed her head
             i almost died myself
             but didn't
           was forced to live
          to give

i was told to do
by some immaculate voice
but to do what i was never told

of course i knew it was to do this
to write these ephemeral things that kept
coming to me
she kept coming to me too

her voice haunting me

her intimate voice singing always in my ear
another presence inside of me
as if she died
        to be reborn complete within me

and to silence her

for i was selfish   you see
i didn't want her to live   even in me

i drank

i drank to silence her
        and when she wouldn't be silenced
        i drank some more
        i drank again for spite
        and in this way over time
        i lost her voice lost my rhyme
and got stuck with this

just drinking
biding time . . .
        see how it happens
        life gets us in these messes

        never wanted it to be like this
        never thought i'd fuck it up so

        but there's no going back
        no starting fresh
        we live once not twice
        don't fuck it up like i fucked up mine
                but do it right
                is my advice

~~~

one day
    her boss, george, pulled her aside
    she was standing outside taking her smoke
    don't get me wrong   i like jim he's a good customer of mine
    but you i love
        you're like a daughter to me
        we've been together many years and i watch you
i think i know you
     like a father   i know your habits
    look you smoke too many of these, he said
             when she lit up a virginia slim
    ever since you've hooked up with him   you are not the same
                  you've changed

you drink more since you've been with him
i know you're broken up about mr ricardo

      it kills you that he left
         but is that why you're doing this
             i say this you see because you're like a
             daughter to me

      that's not true, she said, about ricardo
      his leaving and my staying here   was all mutual
         i haven't thought about him in years

it's only my impression   you see
you've always been sad since ricardo   if that's how you call
him

         and now you seem stuck on this jim
         but what does he do to deserve it
         i only say this you see because you're

like a
daughter to me

i never had a daughter
     all my life   my wife prayed for a daughter
     but only boys
     i had five sons
     but never a daughter
to me   you are my daughter so i care about you
i see you give him money every night

it's our money, george   we practically live together
     my money helps pay the bills   that's all

but you see what i'm saying
     you work so he can sit at the bar and drink

he's working on a poem

sure   sure   it's up to you what you choose to do
i only say this you see because you're like a daughter to me

as to leaving jim
        it wasn't a completely foolish proposition
            the thought had crossed her mind

from time to time
the thought blazed like a periodic comet
lighting the dark sky of her mind

what's more there was
a tiny little voice

which she couldn't quite locate or destroy
though she tried by drinking gin

it started speaking inside of her
the first time jim hit her for no reason
slap across the face
the voice spoke quietly at first
then quietly and persistently

you thought, it said, you could handle this
it was like a song which
        once getting in her ear
                she couldn't shake loose

you thought, it said, you could handle this
you thought, it said, you could handle this

        it spoke to her while she was awake
                and spoke while she was sleeping

you thought, it said, you could handle this

it had happened   when she least expected it
all those previous times were play

but what was this
she had merely said no thank you
      to a proffered drink
      that's when it happened
smart across her face and fierce
brutal was how she described it
      later when she was away from him
         and talking to herself
the contact of the hand against the face
the palm of his hand burning like sandpaper against her face

it was real as bitter reality
and this was followed immediately
by the thought that blazed like a comet
      i should leave him

the tiny little voice went on
you thought, it said, you could handle this
you thought, it said, you could handle this
you thought, it said, you could handle this

slowly the voice added variation
it told her that leaving jim
was her only way out
it would be her salvation
            but sticking with him
                  would lead to ruin and devastation

the tiny mocking voice would pose a question
                        of which direction
                        she preferred to take

                        are you suicidal
                        or do you prefer
                        survival

are you a woman
who is lonely
and in denial

a woman
who prefers
the trial

of jim and drink
to the trial
of facing
the face
of who
you are

and doing
the thing

you daren't think

occasionally the voice would add:

you have lived a whole life prior
to all these hours spent in the tavern

surely you haven't lived to drain
the cup of your time in this dark-lit cavern

every so often   she would hear music
that would make her soften
or see a light at a certain time
of day or night
                       or the flash of a smile across a face
or the smell of lilacs in the spring
for lilacs always had an effect on her
or the feel of an old person's hand   cool and dry
in hers   or a kiss against her cheek
wet and made by a child
                   or the distant sound of canada geese
                          veeing southward
or even once in a while something she read in the paper
and she would say as if waking from a dream: he isn't so bad
he is only jim
he's got his problems
we all do
hell find me a person who doesn't sin

francine would listen to her reason:

my life since i met jim

has been wonderful
i wouldn't change a thing

stick with him and you'll see
was francine's retort

she shows up at the bar
      and worries if   she refuses a drink
he'll give her a clout
or do something vicious like knock her out
      he'd yell, what's wrong   you pregnant
not yet
well then   don't make me drink alone
      he smacks the bar
      come on goddamn it   drink
barkeep two brandies: one neat
one on the rocks

      she sulks   reaches in her pocket
unwraps a candy
        if you want johnny walker red instead just tell me

       no brandy is fine
actually   i'll take an ice water too

       she clears her throat sucks the butterscotch
        and does her best to toe the line
she tells francine   it scares me to think
        of giving all this up
of saying farewell to you and friends like
william the bartender
mallory and louise "the mouse"
sid sheldon rubin ned polski
greta john harry and glen
(who by the way owns that marvelous house in michigan)

even rudy   i'm fond of him
though he was caught

in an embarrassing situation
someone opened the john door

caught him practicing
the fine art of masturbation

he was banned five weeks
from the tavern

but came around when his quarantine
ended

found his spot next to jim
barnacled to the bar he sips his rum

francine listens and urges her to pick up and run
        but run where she asks

where would i go
i've only got home and work

surely there must be more

home and work, francie
        that's all i have
what's more i'm no longer sure
i can quite muster it alone
and the break-up would kill jim

you've become a drunk
        just like him

and it was true

she found she had gotten hooked on drink
found too she needed her newfound friends

she needed a cigarette fix
she needed jim partly for company partly for sex

but mostly for company someone to sit with
while drinking i'll take that cigarette

i'll take my brandy too
while you're at it where's my water and ice

jim smokes and stares ahead of him
she tries to be nice smoking drinking

she remembers how she had tried
           to give up smoking in the past

           at first she thought it'd be easy
           quit smokes be a little queasy
           she could handle that
           so off she rode cold turkey
           every one at the diner joking
it wouldn't be long till she'd be smoking
not long at all
there was nothing special
about her willpower
she tried to prove every one wrong
           started popping her candy
           i've more mettle than these people
           she liked to think

           and things like smoking cures
           are crazy   it's cold turkey or
           nothing

it all changed when
a simple test came up positive
she checked it twice

lo

and reeled in
a pregnancy

she who
since ricardo
		grew less and less certain
		about ever bearing children

became suddenly a harbor
for two:	a girl
		a boy

such joy

she closed her eyes and left the harbor
to swim the open sea of her pregnancy

her pregnancy		a sea change not of water or whiskey
as jim would have it

but of pure joy
		no other way of stating it

she swam
		and swam her arms outstretched upon the pure joy sea

			and when she tired she floated

unfettered and free

gaze into the tunnels of my eyes and be lost
in a windblown world of breaking hopes
and a shipwrecked country
of green-blue dreams. . . .

she wanted to sing a song again
    a song
        not of rain
        but of buoyancy

o what a stupid thing to say
    she looked herself in the mirror to see
        if it was really she who was saying such things

but it was true

for how else to put it
words can't express how i feel
    i look no different
everything is exactly the same
work   home   jim

but now when i stand out of doors
taking a breather from work
my foot   propped against the wall
i feel as if the other is dangled
in the current of cool life
its waters rushing through my toes
no more virginia slims
no more sins nor gin mixed with tonic

she stands outdoors to breath the fragrant air
                        and feels a touch demonic

when she serves her customers
       she serves them just the same
       as she has served them all before
nothing has changed
yet everything is changed

do you know what is happening to me
    she wants to grab anyone near
    and tell them of her secret
    wants to buttonhole
        seize the lapel
    of her nearest customer
    but so far she didn't dare to tell anyone
    she doesn't even tell jim

    he wouldn't even understand
    it was best to keep this thing to herself a while

                    all those years
her life yoked
as if it were a plow
she pulled through the barren fields of her days
all those years the dust of time kicked up and barren
dragging the plow
                              up and down the restaurant floor
                              dragging it even to the feet of jim
                    she had felt so pathetic when she met him
                    and all these months past getting lost in gin

      but this pregnancy reversed this weight

she felt like an astronaut or rather the mothership
she imagined her child umbilically attached
like a space walker moving among the stars
she imagined sputnik   she imagined mars

other days she imagined her body a ship at sea
her belly tilted downward like a keel
her hair catching the wind like a mainsail
all her days floating in a sea of joy
and her babies safe in the hollows of her ship
made her days seem effortless
her life seemed
penetrated by shafts of light

for a long time after she conceived
she would say
apropos of nothing
oh to be light
to be infinitesimally light
to be light with infants

a boy a girl
such joy

she lost the boy
in the sixth week

and was shattered
        she bled for six more days
        and was sure it was the daughter
        draining out of her
        but the girl hung in
        and slowly her grief for the boy
            subsided and she rediscovered her early joy

after all
it wasn't the worst case scenario
she was pregnant
what's more she had always wanted a girl

she thought she would name the girl anne
anne was the name of every strong woman in her family
going back three generations
        there were four annes in total
        each of whom had taken a stand
        she wished
        that she had been named anne
        and had collected some of their strength

she tried to leave him once
        she doesn't know exactly why she tried to leave him
                it was all a big mistake
                        he showed up at her apartment
                        and made her pay
                        he was in a drunken rage
                        o the drunken rage for order
                he struck her once across the face
                then kicked her when she was down
        broke a rib
        and with that it was ended

----
a flock of swallows rises up from the trees
      a flock rises from the trees by the lake
      a flock of swallows rises
forms and reforms in the shape
            of the trees they had nested in by the lake
      the flock rising
                  guided by the memory of trees
        it flies in the shape of a tree

she too is guided
by a memory she swears she will never forget
      she remembers it now standing by the dumpster
      and marvels at how time has gone past
      it's five years since
             jim o'connor has died

a funeral fit for a king
she'd never seen anything like it
before or since
the crowded pews at church
the lengthy eulogies telling the news of who jim was
and what they said of him made her feel
she had met him too late
     and missed out on a better jim
     even his brother chris got up to the lectern
          and told of jim's many adventures
          going all the way back to those early days
          when jim had been pinned beneath his bike
          and burned
          chris even pulled out

and read that poem of the turtle for all to hear
some later commented how nearly chris resembled jim

gretchen was asked if she had anything she wanted to add
she demurred
chose instead to sit far back in the church

anonymous
and listen to the stories of who jim was

jim had been the resident
        bard
        a poet who liked to quote
                poetry
                who liked to make quips

        this was the gist of what the eulogists said
        but no mention was made of anne burroughs
                how she died
                or what role jim had played

they talked instead of how he died
he was forty-eight
           dying of a bad heart
           but he didn't let that stop him
           after open heart he returned with his surgeon
           to the bar toasted him with a raised glass

next day he stripped down naked near the lake
           and   diving   went for a swim

when the eulogies were done
they all filed past   paid their final respects
bagpipers two fiddle players the irish drum
                    and a solemn ceremony followed at the cemetery
                    a hole was dug
                    the casket lowered
                    vows were made   he'd never be forgotten
as if a ship or newborn yacht were launched upon the sea
against his casket rudy smashed a fifth of bourbon whiskey
he bid his friend adieu

in the hole the notes for his unfinished poem—his epic—were
scattered
a few prayers said   followed by a moment of quietude

that's when she looked up   saw the flock of swallows rise from
the tree
she marveled at how they kept
the shape of the tree even as they flew in flight
she turned her head again and clods of dirt came raining down
the undertaker stood near the pile of dirt
          he was wearing   yellow
          wellingtons   his silver spade cleaved the hill of dirt
the dirt fell   raining
skittering down

                    clattering the hard hood of his casket
                    the great soft lumps   clods of earth falling
                    burying once and for all jim

~~~

her daughter was born with a full head of flaxen hair
    a towhead named anne
    and later nicknamed flaxen-anne
    she never knew the man who made her
    he perished months before she was born
    it was said he had only gone for a swim
    he stood on the limestone ripraps
    hottest day of the hell-hot summer
    stripped himself and leaped quick into the water
    leaped as if he were a retriever hunting ducks
or as if he were some madman diving to meet his maker
    he dove because he saw on the heat-hazed horizon
    a mirage-made freshwater whale
    no one else had ever seen such a thing as this
    nothing like it since the monster of loch ness

he saw too his destiny coming into focus
        but he who was destined to do something big
        saw the whale and realized it was his time to do
        this is what he had been singled out for
        not poetry—poems be damned—
        not drink—neither to be the owner of a yacht—
        a public bard nor tender of a bar
        his mission suddenly clear
        was to swim free of all debt and debris

as he lost breath and started sinking
        he remembered a poem from long ago
        and quoted each line with each new stroke
            defiant as he sank
and as he sank
the poem sank with him:

you are flaxen haired and the night is long
soldiers plunder their dead

they lie in their fields
pockets turned out

their eyes stopper the gas
that builds—builds—inside of them

why did they leave home
so young for the trenches

why did they leave home so young
when the flaxen haired girl told them: no,

don't go, my hair is flaxen
the night is long, stay home

just then the thought occurred to him
    the futility of what we do

WHO READS THIS SHIT ANYWAYS
AND WHAT THE HELL IS THE POINT

like that
    it was done

later when anne was older
she wanted to know about her father
what was he like, she asked mom

not nearly as fine as you. . . .

seriously, mom,   she pleaded
tell me
well, she said
if you must know the truth
he was a poet
an oral poet to boot
so nothing really exists for you to see

yes i know but what else can you tell me

only this:
    that one day when he was sober
        he did something quite remarkable

        we were sitting on a wall
            fishing at the harbor

        when he turned his eyes back
            impossible to describe what that was like

        only it was astonishing
            to see someone so ordinary
                as him

        become—how else say it—a sort of
            vessel through which a voice
                of elemental force

        was transmitted

some thought it was a party trick
    your father summoning voices from beyond

it was anything but a trick
    it was unsettling
        unsettling the way
        an epileptic fit is unsettling

        but also rather beautiful
        what those voices he channeled said

i don't remember much of his poem
but i do recall this line
about a whale
it has always stuck in my mind
it went something like this

    there was a whale swimming out on the lake's horizon
her snout was covered with whale lice
and she swam gracefully at a slow lumbering velocity

that's about it
    and the feeling   your father always carried with him
        that his talent for channeling voices was wasted

~~~

at three in the afternoon
planes crisscrossing overhead

leaving o'hare airport and heading east
for new york city or god knows where

on one of the hottest days of the dog-day summer
with heat-stricken people

collecting in lines behind the bubblers
drawing water into parched throats

or into empty plastic bottles pouring it
onto heads shoulders necks and backs

and heat-fatigued runners
panting pounding their feet on the pavement

and bikers of all sorts pedaling in tandem
or single

some leaned forward for speed some sitting back for comfort
others trailing recumbent children in nylon

covered carts and bladers and kids on scooters
or skateboards and frisbees tossed in the air

while dogs in the park bark at squirrels
they bark at crows cawing in the treetops

bark at the crowds of people gathering in the park
the dog owners talk amongst themselves

the picnickers arrive and collect on blankets
fold-up chairs they swing from hammocks slung

between the trunks of trees the smell of charcoal smoke
drifts on the hot summer air and is co-mingled

with the smell of fire-charred porkchops
pork ribs chicken barbecue sauce hamburgers

and hot dogs which are turned slowly by fork
pricked and cut cooked and served on a bun

the sweet split overripe watermelon
is cracked open or cut in slices it spills

forth its cool pink fruit and god how sweet
the juice dripping down the arms off the elbows

onto pants or skirts or bare naked thigh and knee
the spit seed spit arching into the air by kids

the trash refuse and detritus of picnickers
accumulates and scatters about the park it collects

in the chain-link fences on the branches of bushes
and look there blowing upon the breeze

empty potato chip bags cellophane wrappers
pieces of paper drift slowly or blow

upon the hot wind this debris carried on a current of rising air
the lazily stirring breeze bearing

all this refuse upward aloft into
the long arms of maples oaks mulberries

cottonwoods buckeyes dogwoods magnolias
or back out onto the lake the pristine lake

beautiful lake michigan long since sullied
by days and years of this and now

another summer day's trash is borne away
to sully it more and the sound

of a hundred radios playing
can you hear them

boom boxes and djs with
makeshift stages twisting their turntables

and speakers banging out a sort of wild
inchoate sound gospel rap blues

country talk radio even vivaldi punctuated
by some shrill religious minister

shouting hellfire from the sky

—prepare yourself for he is coming
and when he comes he shall come
with a scythe in hand and cull those who
have turned their eyes away
he shall strike them down
separate the grain from the chaff
the devil lives in merchandise
in nike high-top shoes illicit drugs
he lives in adultery bestiality overripe sexuality
if you turn your eyes away
from him . . . fire fire fire
for you and your eyes are made of clay—

from all these speakers in the park
there reverberates a definable bass beat

akin to the rhythm of the heart
it thump thumps lending a sort of rhythm

to this hot summer day marking this time as our time
this place as our place like mayflies

we have come forth from the froth
from the ether from nothingness into being

to do our life's dance
beneath the circuit of sun stars and moon

we have come to mate perchance to dream
perchance not and die

perchance peacefully
perchance not so peacefully

nor will we know the how
nor why it unfolds in such and such a way

bestowing pain and suffering to some
and to some a sort of blithe catatonic bliss

this the time not of our ancestors nor the time
which shall be the time of our children's children

but this our time and now ours
what shall we do with it

but sing a little song
sing a song to the selfsame rhythm of the park

of promontory point—a great
expanse of lawn jutting like a camel's hump

into the lake's waters—a promontory
artificially made from landfill

trucked in by wpa workers
hemmed in by carved limestone blocks which had

been cut and hewn from the quarries of indiana
wisconsin stacked like blocks

to stem erosion and meet head-on
the heavings of storms and waves

so that now after some seventy years those
same limestone blocks

lie scattered as if tossed by
a giant's hand—they lay there toppled

astray upended like miniatures
of stonehenge and where they lie

bathers now recline
in the heat swimmers lie sunning

drying themselves after a swim
in the cold lake water

one by one they come
starting early in the morning

up with the sun with the starlings the robins
the sparrows the grackles the crows

up with the industrious south american
parrots that were set free from a pet shop

and now miraculously have found a way
to eke out an existence this far north

of their native land
and who would have believed

a small colony of parrots
could survive here on the south side of chicago

and now they too take shelter in the shade
of tall oaks on this the hottest day of the year

they hide in the high sooty branches
their towering nests ten feet high

and down below taxicabs
and public buses ambulances cop cars

pedestrian traffic cruise the streets
women with children in strollers

men with children in strollers
the infirm in wheelchairs parked

in the shade tossing seeds or crumbs
to the pigeons and whole squadrons

of pigeons descending from the skies
quibbling over crumbs they rise

to the skies again where they cut
their arc and a man and woman

screw in the bushes
missionary style

a woman and a man argue
over something and the cars

every one of them a chevy
a buick or a toyota a mercedes benz

or range rover with bass beat thumping
to a rhythm akin to the heart

and here and there they drive
and the lord loves them

—the good lord died on the cross
for each and every one of you
and the good lord is dying on
the cross today for you and armageddon
is around the corner
if you look close even a bit
of armageddon may be found in you

and so it comes raining down
out of the sky this great din filtered

through radio street corner megaphone
shouted through hands to any and all

and gospel music that's sung with a passion
and god it'll break your heart

the pretty little girls singing for all they're worth
until it's not even noticed that a man

half-drunk strips down naked
and dives off a limestone rock

dives like a boy dives he dives
with limber grace and with limber grace

begins to swim his arms like scissors
cutting the surface of the water

as if it were blue gift wrap a sheen
of summer light shimmers off the surface

he swims methodically out to
the heat-hazed horizon

in search of the whale which swims
stirring the calm water with its fin

swears he sees it there then swims toward it
between the shadow and the wave

there swims the whale the breath of the whale
is released into the air with a great sigh

the whale emerges from the deep its terrible eye
takes it all in—takes this scene—chicago

takes it all in comprehending it with
its enormous eye with enormous

serenity the whale swims
in the lake this though

a great lake yet without a tide
untied to the rhythms of the moon

and all day it swims unnoticed
and all night it swims unnoticed

until it is noticed by him
and off he dives then swims to the whale.

JOSEPH G. PETERSON works in publishing. He is the author of the critically acclaimed novel, *Beautiful Piece*. *Inside the Whale: A Novel in Verse* is his second book, and his third novel, *Wanted: Elevator Man*, will be published by Northern Illinois University Press in the spring of 2012. He lives in Chicago with his wife and two daughters.